DOCTOR · WHO

THE DARKSMITH LEGACY

BBC CHILDREN'S BOOKS
Published by the Penguin Group
Penguin Books Ltd, 80 Strand, London, WC2R 0RL, England
Penguin Group (USA) Inc., 375 Hudson Street, New York 10014, USA
Penguin Books (Australia) Ltd, 250 Camberwell Road, Camberwell, Victoria 3124, Australia
(A division of Pearson Australia Group Pty Ltd)
Canada, India, New Zealand, South Africa
Published by BBC Children's Books, 2009
Text and design © Children's Character Books, 2009
Written by Colin Brake
Cover illustration by Peter McKinstry
10 9 8 7 6 5 4 3 2 1
ISBN: 978-1-40590-514-5
Printed in Great Britain by Clays Ltd, St Ives plc

DOCTOR·WHO

THE DARKSMITH LEGACY

THE GRAVES OF MORDANE

BY **COLIN BRAKE**

Book
2

Contents

The Story So far . . .

A few years into our future... The Doctor arrives on the Moon where Professor Dollund and his team are surveying for possible mining sites, but mysterious statues made of dust have begun to attack his survey team. The Doctor discovers that the lunar dust is somehow alive, animated by a powerful Crystal of unknown origin.

Far away on the planet of Karagula, the Darksmith Collective dispatches a robot Agent to recover their Eternity Crystal.

Back on the Moon, the Doctor manages to place the Crystal in a stasis box, cutting it off from the outside world and leaves it in the TARDIS while he checks on Dollund and his people. But when he returns the TARDIS has been taken away on a Moon buggy.

Following the buggy, the Doctor arrives in a hangar where the Darksmith Collective's Agent is waiting...

The Dead Planet

angar 7 was a vast open space. Standing alone and abandoned inside the hangar was a Moon Buggy. The Doctor smiled with delight. But as he approached, the smile faded to a frown. The Buggy's cargo deck was empty.

The Doctor could see the dusty outline where something had been standing – something square and the exact size of the TARDIS. But it had gone now. The Doctor looked round, hoping to see someone he could ask where the TARDIS had been taken.

There was only one figure in sight. A robot built of metal and plastic. It walked with an elegance and speed that was surprising.

'Oh, hi,' the Doctor said as the robot approached. 'Look at you, someone took pride in their work, didn't they. You are beautiful, you know that? What engineering. What design. What – *are you doing*?!'

The Doctor's voice had become a strangled yelp as the robot hauled him off his feet. It lifted the Doctor into the air, then hurled him aside. The Doctor crashed painfully into the Moon Buggy, and slumped to the ground. He shook his head groggily, wondering what was going on. 'Was it something I said?' he muttered.

The robot was looming over him. Metal fingers snapped viciously as it reached down for the Doctor. Its voice was an echoing metallic boom.

'Brother Varlos – I have found you at last,' it grated. 'You have been tried in your absence, and sentenced to death.'

The Doctor twisted quickly and rolled over a few times before scrambling to his feet. The robot, although it looked heavy and slow, was just as quick. The Doctor began to run but the robot was immediately on his heels. With nowhere to hide the Doctor turned and stopped suddenly, holding his hands out. 'Wait,' he shouted, 'there's been a mistake.'

To his relief the robot did as it was asked and

stopped in its tracks.

'Mistake?' the booming voice asked.

The Doctor nodded, gasping for breath. 'Mistaken identity. I'm not Brother Varlow...'

'Brother Varlos,' the robot corrected him.

'Or him,' muttered the Doctor. 'I'm the Doctor.'

'The Eternity Crystal was here. Only Brother Varlos knew where the Crystal was therefore you must be Brother Varlos.'

'Wait, wait, wait...' the Doctor stammered quickly. 'Stop and think a moment. Your logic is flawed.'

The robot said nothing. The Doctor looked into the cold metallic face – humanoid but alien. Through a plastic panel at the top of the head he could see the tiny flashes of light as the positronic brain of the creature examined billions of possibilities at incredible speeds. If only he could see what it was thinking as clearly.

'I don't know what the Eternity Crystal is,' the Doctor continued. 'Tell me about it, perhaps I can help.'

The robot tilted his head as if considering.

'The Eternity Crystal is powerful and dangerous,'

the booming metallic voice explained. 'Too dangerous to be left here on this dead Moon. After the Mordane incident my masters decreed that it must never be allowed to leave their care again until their contract is completed.'

The Doctor took a step or two backwards. 'I don't know what you're talking about. Mordane, the Eternity Crystal, I've never heard of them.' He looked around the vast emptiness of Hangar 7. 'Don't suppose you've seen a big blue box, by any chance?' he asked, casually. The robot said nothing.

'This Brother Varlos you're looking for — what does he actually look like?' the Doctor wondered.

The robot seemed to be considering whether or not to answer the Doctor's questions. Finally it began to speak again. 'He is old, grey-haired...'

'Old, well, that's relative, but grey-haired? Take a close look,' the Doctor invited the giant robot. 'And scan me. Listen - two hearts! How many does Varlos have?'

'Analysing!' the booming voice announced and then the robot seemed to freeze. The Doctor took another couple of steps away, experimentally. The robot didn't seem to notice. Not taking his eyes off the robot the Doctor backed away with greater confidence.

In a distant galaxy on the planet Mordane, three brave humans were walking through the biggest cemetery in known space. Mordane was, literally, a planet of the dead. It had been used for centuries by the space-faring peoples of a thousand worlds. The entire surface of the planet was covered by cemeteries and catacombs, the final resting place for the much loved dead of over a hundred different species.

'I suppose at least we know now why the planet was declared off limits,' said the youngest of the party, a pretty girl of about sixteen who liked to be called Catz, although her real name was Caroline.

The eldest of the group, a tough-looking women with a well-lined face snorted with derision. 'That's going to help me sleep at night!' she commented sarcastically and stomped ahead.

'Don't worry about Captain Gomez,' first officer Chandra told the young girl sympathetically. 'She just wants to find what we need so we can get off this place.'

The three of them continued in silence, moving between the long rows of gravestones towards the mausolea ahead of them. This was Sector Alpha, on the continent given over to human remains. As well as thousands and thousands of regular graves there were also numerous family mausolea and catacombs in which thousands of other dead humans were enjoying the endless sleep of death. Except, as Captain Gomez and her two companions had discovered when their ship had crashed here two days ago, the 'sleep' was not as endless as they had been led to believe.

'We need to make camp,' announced the Captain. Chandra nodded and slipped his heavy rucksack from his back. Catz watched as the rucksack expanded, on command, unfolding itself into a massive tent that secured itself to the ground and to nearby gravestones. The plastic looked flimsy but Catz knew that when the right signal was activated it would solidify into a protective shell that would keep out any hostile forces. This was the third night that she would be grateful for the protection of the Intelligent Plastic Survival Pod.

'It's nearly dark,' Chandra told her. 'Get inside before it starts.'

Catz clambered into the tent, and Chandra followed her. She looked behind her to see Captain

Gomez staring back at the sinking sun. 'Can you see anything Captain?' asked Chandra. Gomez nodded and then turned and hurried to join them inside the tent. Chandra operated the sonic control and the door sealed itself. Gomez looked at her two companions with a serious expression.

'It's starting,' she told them.

After escaping from the robot Agent's gaze, the Doctor had found a base computer and with a little encouragement from the sonic screwdriver he had managed to access the security camera records for the entire complex. The Moon Base was a series of atmosphere and gravity controlled domes linked by underground tunnels and surface passageways, all scattered around the central spaceport area. The security footage showed the robot Agent commandeering a loading robot and sending the TARDIS to the hold of a cargo freighter, where it was packed alongside crates of mineral samples to return to Earth. The Doctor noticed with horror that the freighter was scheduled to take off in ten minutes time. Desperately he called up a graphic showing the layout of the base to look for the quickest route to the freighter.

Activity

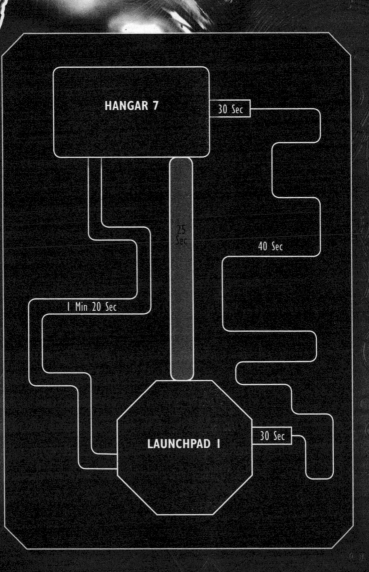

HANGAR 7

30 Sec

25 Sec

40 Sec

1 Min 20 Sec

LAUNCHPAD 1

30 Sec

ROCK TYPE

- **Route A**   Underground passage. No Gravity.
              Average speed: 2 metres per second.
              Distance 50 metres.

- **Route B**   Buggy. No Gravity.
              Average speed 10 metres per second. But
              airlock takes 30 seconds on entry and exit.
              Distance 400 metres.

- **Route C**   Over ground link way.
              Artificial Gravity – Earth Normal.
              Average Speed: 3 metres per second.
              Distance 240 metres.

Fastest Route... Calculating.

Which route will get the Doctor to his
destination in the shortest time?

'Final loading complete, launch imminent. All crew to launch positions.' The automatic tannoy voice blared out of hidden speakers as the Doctor stumbled into the cargo freighter. Using the Buggy would have been easier than running through the overground pathway but the airlock delay would have made him too late.

To his relief he could see the familiar sight of the TARDIS, nestled amongst other less colourful boxes. Now he could get into the TARDIS and take the time to have a closer look at that Crystal. The words of the robot Agent rang in his ears. What was the Eternity Crystal? And who were the mysterious 'Masters' who had sent the remarkable and persistent robot Agent to collect it?

The Doctor started walking towards the TARDIS but then stopped as a giant figure stepped out of hiding behind adjacent boxes to block the doors. It was the robot Agent.

'I have not concluded my business with you,' it announced and took a menacing step towards the Doctor.

The Stowaway

Catz tried to sleep as best she could but it was difficult. The intelligent plastic tent surface had formed a comfortable mattress inside her sleeping area so she didn't have to sleep on the cold ground, but despite the relative comfort of the bed surface it was hard to sleep for long. It wasn't anything inside the tent keeping her awake – it was all the activity outside. The 'dead' world of Mordane was far from still after nightfall.

There were bangs and crashes all night as the creatures outside threw themselves and anything else they could find at the tent, desperate to get to the living creatures within. No-one wanted to think about where they had come from. During the day they saw no-one and nothing, not even an animal or an insect; truly it was a dead planet. But at night, everything was different.

Catz glanced over at her companions. Captain Gomez was sprawled out on her bed, fast asleep and snoring loudly. In other circumstances Catz might have found the sight amusing; the grumpy Captain lying with her mouth open making the most appalling snorting noises but, with the constant sounds of attack from outside, the Captain's snores were strangely reassuring. Jitan Chandra was completely different. He was sitting in a fixed cross-legged position with his arms folded and his eyes closed. He wasn't asleep, as such, but in a deep mediation. He had told Catz that he found this form of rest to be more productive than sleep and, true to his word, each morning he had 'woken' full of energy.

Satisfied that both her companions were unable to see what she was doing, Catz pulled out her tiny laptop. She flipped open the lid and activated the screen, tapping a few quick instructions with the interface wand. A graphic appeared showing the area they had covered that day, confirming they were on the right path. In the morning she would have to suggest that they try looking in the catacombs. With any luck they'd reach her goal soon.

'Hello there, long time no see. Good to see you again,' the Doctor spoke rapidly hoping to engage the robot in conversation before it began tossing him around like a Frisbee as it had done when they first met.

'Analysis complete,' the robot announced. 'You are not Brother Varlos.'

The Doctor smiled. 'Well, there you go, what did I say, eh? Glad we sorted that out. Take care then, see you around.' The Doctor made as if to slip past the robot but, without warning, it extended its arm in a flash of motion and the Doctor found himself almost knocked to the ground as his chest barrelled into the unflinching metal limb. 'Ooof!' he exclaimed, as he had the breath knocked out of him.

'There is still the matter of the Eternity Crystal,' the robot reminded the Doctor.

'The Crystal?' the Doctor echoed, playing for time.

'The Crystal was here, on this Moon. It was active. It animated dust.' The robot's description made it sound so simple, so natural. But for the Doctor and the members of the survey team it had been a nightmare, until the Doctor locked the Crystal in a stasis box safely hidden inside the TARDIS and everything had returned to normal.

'The trace signal ends at a previously detected location of this blue box,' the robot Agent continued. 'The blue box that belongs to you.'

'This old thing?' commented the Doctor, patting the wooden frame with one hand. 'Yes it's a sort of mobile store cupboard, I've got lots of bits and bobs in there. Singing Sand from Sarpanto Two, a bottle of G'uu Water from the Spa of Old Rusoon, stick of rock from Blackpool, all sorts of rubbish... So tell me about this Crystal then.'

The robot regarded him with its cold blank visual receptors. The artificial lenses contracted as it considered its response.

'The Eternity Crystal was fashioned by Brother Varlos many years ago. It is the heart of his greatest creation.'

'And what was that then?' asked the Doctor, his curiosity getting the better of him.

'I cannot say,' confessed the robot. 'But the Crystal is both powerful and dangerous and must be returned to my Masters. I demand access to your box.' The robot curled his arm around the Doctor pulling him tight against his metallic side. 'Co-operate or I will crush you.'

With the coming of dawn and a new day's light from the powerful and youthful star that Mordane orbited, the mysterious activity of the night ceased and peace returned to the endless graveyards of the planet of the dead. Captain Gomez had checked that it was safe to emerge from the tent and then gave the order to break camp. As quickly – and as cleverly – as it had unfolded itself, the intelligent plastic contracted and reformed into the rucksack shape that first officer Chandra wore on his back. The Captain's rucksack contained survival packs of food and water and, after a brief but satisfying breakfast, the trio were ready to continue their search.

'We're never going to find the stuff we need to make the repair here,' Catz suggested. 'I mean, some of the gravestones have got some metal embellishments but not what we need.'

'The girl's right, Captain,' Jitan pitched in. 'We need a different strategy.'

The Captain was grim-faced as she scanned the area around them in an arc. Her handheld scanner beeped and the screen filled with details. 'Significant metal in two areas,' she announced, 'five or so clicks in that direction,' she indicated with her arm. 'Or in the opposite direction but underground.'

'We've no digging tools, Captain,' Chandra reminded her.

'We don't need them,' Catz piped up, pleased of the opportunity. 'I think there are catacombs over where you said there was an underground signal.' The Captain looked at her with cold eyes. 'Underground burial chambers,' Catz added.

'I know what catacombs are,' the Captain told her coldly. 'I'm just not sure I want to be caught in them when nightfall comes.'

'It's a short day on this planet,' Chandra interceded, reminding Catz of the facts, 'but we've got at least six hours until nightfall.'

Catz looked at the Captain and tried to smile winningly. 'Your decision, of course, Captain.'

'Let me go, crushing me won't get you into my box will it?' the Doctor demanded. A moment later the robot released him. The Doctor took the opportunity to take a step closer to the TARDIS. The Robot spun around, ready to spring into action.

The Doctor held out a hand. 'Wait, it's all right, no need to panic.'

'Panic is not part of my programming,' commented the robot.

'Good for you,' muttered the Doctor. 'Now take a look at the size of my box. It's a bit cramped in there, and I'm not likely to slip out the back door.' The Doctor lied easily, crossing his fingers behind his back. 'So maybe it's best if you let me go and fetch this Crystal for you, eh? If I'm not back in a couple of minutes, well you can probably smash your way in after me, OK?'

The robot considered for a moment and then slowly nodded its head.

Relieved the Doctor bounded to the door, unlocked and opened it just a fraction, not wanting the robot to see too much of the interior. 'Won't be a tick,' he promised and quickly slipped inside, slamming the door shut behind him.

Once inside the TARDIS the Doctor bounded up the gangway to the central console and began running around, setting controls. 'Right then,' he muttered to himself, 'we'll lock the temporal brakes, don't want to travel in time this trip, and set the co-ordinates for mysterious Mordane.'

Outside the robot Agent waited patiently. The Crystal was inside the blue box and soon it would be in his possession. Suddenly an unearthly noise filled the air; a rasping, scraping sound. At the same moment the light fixed on the roof of the blue box began to flash. Something was happening. The robot Agent jumped forward, arms outstretched and grabbed hold of the box with his powerful arms. Clinging on tightly to the box he noticed that the interior of the cargo hold around him was fading away and a moment later he was somewhere else. He was still holding on to the blue box, which was now spinning at impossible speeds through the vacuum of deep space.

The Awakening

The Captain looked at her scanner. 'Something new,' she announced, 'some huge energy surge, over there.' To Catz's relief the Captain was pointing in exactly the direction she wanted to go - towards the entrance to the catacombs.

'What are we waiting for?' she asked. 'Let's go and investigate.'

'Wait,' ordered the Captain, stowing the scanner in her rucksack. She pulled two hand weapons from deep within the bag and threw one to Chandra. 'Let's not take any chances.'

Chandra nodded and weighed the gun in his hand, flicking the safety catch to the off position. 'Ready when you are.'

The forces buffeting the robot Agent as he clung

to the wooden box were unimaginable. First, the TARDIS had spun through the vacuum of Deep Space and then through the nightmare reality of the Space-Time Vortex, where concepts such as 'here' and 'now' lost all meaning. All through this incredible journey the Agent's metallic fingers had gripped tight, keeping the powerful figure hugging the TARDIS. Now, as the space and time craft approached the surface of the planet Mordane, it spun even faster.

Even the advanced technology of the Darksmiths had its limits. First one finger and then another came loose and a moment later the whole left hand of the robot came clear of the blue box. Before he could grab hold again the whirling action of the machine hurled him backwards and his remaining hand couldn't hold his weight.

The robot fell, heating up as he accelerated towards the surface of the planet. Internal sensors told the robot's positronic brain that the surface temperatures of his skin were approaching their tolerance limit. The Darksmiths had designed their Agent well but they couldn't protect him from such intense heat.

His in-built teleport device was his only hope

of survival but with no data on the arrival point a teleport could be just as deadly as the heat. Quickly scanning the ground, the Agent calculated his teleport co-ordinates and activated the teleport. A human might have crossed his fingers for luck – the artificial intelligence inside the Agent merely calculated his chances of survival and came up with the figure... sixty-five per cent.

Inside the TARDIS the Doctor skipped around the central console, flipping switches as the sound of the engines began to fade away. It hadn't been the smoothest of landings; in fact the Doctor wasn't too happy with the entire journey. Something had been off, something had made the trip even more erratic than usual – at least up until the final materialisation – but the Doctor couldn't work out what the problem had been. Still, the journey was over now and the TARDIS was standing on the surface of Mordane - the Planet of the Dead.

On the TARDIS scanner the Doctor could see a number of shrines and memorials dotted along a hillside. In the valley below, row after row of gravestones decorated the slopes. Lines of bright, white headstones surrounded by vivid green grass.

Apart from the vegetation there was no sign of life anywhere; just plenty of signs of death. The Doctor reminded himself that this was, after all, a planet of cemeteries. What else would he expect to find here? He wondered what the Agent had meant by the 'Mordane incident.'

The Doctor flicked off the data bank. Maybe he was about to find out why the planet had been placed off limits.

'Come on then Doctor,' he said aloud, wishing not for the first time recently that he wasn't travelling alone. 'Only one way to solve the mystery.'

He stopped and looked at the stasis box in which he had placed the Eternity Crystal. Whatever had happened here was connected to the Crystal somehow, he was sure, but how? He slipped the stasis box into one of his incredibly deep pockets and headed for the door to the outside world. 'At least I'm not going to step out of the door and run in trouble for once,' he muttered to himself before opening the inner door of the TARDIS and stepping out onto the surface of Mordane.

'Put your hands up,' called out a voice. It was a voice that sounded human, female and one that was clearly used to being obeyed when it gave an order.

'Then again...' he whispered to himself.

The Doctor quickly pulled the TARDIS door shut behind him and raised his arms as requested.

'Don't shoot,' he called out, 'I'm harmless.'

'We'll be the judge of that,' replied the voice which had spoken before. And now a figure stepped out of hiding behind a nearby memorial. It was a woman in a slightly dirty uniform with Captain's stripes on the shoulders. She was carrying a gun. To the Doctor's eyes she looked to be in her fifties. She carried herself with authority but there was a slight tremble to her hand where she held the weapon.

'Search him,' she ordered and two more characters emerged from the shadows. A teenage girl with mischievous eyes, and a darker skinned young man in a similar uniform to the Captain. The man passed his weapon to the girl – who looked very uncomfortable with it – and patted down the Doctor.

'There's really no need,' he assured them, 'I never carry weapons.'

'What's this then?' asked the man, holding up a slim metallic torch-like object that he had found in

TARDIS
Data Bank
Mordane –
Planet of the Dead

- First Planet of the Star System Gandii Prime

- Age: Approx 16 billion years

- Diameter: 2,678 km

Mordane is a small planet spinning at high velocity around a class three red giant star. Each day on Mordane is ten hours long. In winter months the days in the Northern Hemisphere can be as little as two hours long, with eight hours of darkness.

For centuries Mordane has been a Cemetery Planet.

Planetary civilisations from a thousand worlds have travelled to Mordane to bury their dead with respect. Death rites from many different cultures are represented on Mordane and there are numerous variations in the way the dead are laid to rest on the planet.

Each of the planet's three major land masses is divided into a dozen different sectors, with each sector assigned to a particular race, species, or planet.

Humans from the Colony worlds of Folflower, Mayside, Riverville, Wystone and Humberville have been buried here for over four hundred years. Some of the dead are placed in regular graves, dug precisely six feet under the surface. Others are in individual tombs. In a number of sectors there are extensive catacombs and each sector had a major Necropolis, consisting of tombs, memorials and mausolea.

Approximately 80 years ago Mordane was declared a grade two quarantine world and all contact was forbidden by Galactic Law. No reason has been recorded for the quarantine ruling.

the Doctor's coat pocket.

'Sonic screwdriver,' explained the Doctor, 'not a weapon just a really useful tool. A high-tech update of the Swiss Army knife. It's even got a setting for removing stones from horse's hooves.'

'Are you some kind of engineer?' the girl asked, taking a step closer.

The Doctor smiled, taking in the sight of the three of them, the state of their clothes and the dirt on the faces. He was rapidly putting two and two together and making what he hoped was four. 'Problem with your space craft?' he asked. 'Crash landing, was it? Couple of days ago?'

The dark-skinned man was looking at the Doctor open-mouthed. 'How did you know? Have you been tracking us?' he demanded.

'Don't be a fool Chandra, he's just arrived here, hasn't he?' the Captain pointed out. The Captain shoved the gun into her belt and reached out her hand. 'Captain Gomez, of the good ship Elizabeth the Fourth,' she said. The Doctor took the extended hand and shook it firmly. 'I'm the Doctor,' he told them, 'perhaps I can help you.'

The robot Agent lay at the bottom of a deep trench.

Its heavy metal and plastic body had ploughed through the topsoil of a stretch of hillside, yet to be covered with memorials, like a hot knife slicing through butter. For the moment the body lay there as inert and lifeless as the corpses in the billions of graves on Mordane. But then a spark of life flickered deep within the alien mechanisms encased in the armoured body and the robot rebooted itself.

In seconds the mechanical creature executed a complete self-scan. The results were remarkable given the speed with which he had hit the ground. The unit had sustained major impact damage but nothing that couldn't be repaired. The robot Agent had been designed to overcome such minor injuries as these; self-repair systems were part of every component within its mechanical body. It would just be a matter of time and then the Agent would be able to continue his pursuit of the mysterious Doctor and reclaim the Eternity Crystal.

Unaware that the robot Agent had managed to hitch a lift on the TARDIS the Doctor was being brought up to speed by Captain Gomez and her companions. As they talked, the four of them began to move towards the massive monument that led to the catacombs.

'So what happened to your spaceship?' asked the Doctor, when they told him about their crash landing.

'I wish I knew,' confessed Chandra, 'there was a sudden loss of power.'

'But you've no idea of the cause?' the Doctor persisted.

Chandra shrugged. 'There must have been a power surge, it burnt out the engine thrust regulator.'

'But all we need is some trisilicate and Mr Chandra can make a new one, can't you?' said Catz with a hopeful smile.

Chandra shot her a quick look. 'With a bit of luck,' he commented.

Captain Gomez, a few metres ahead of the rest of them, snorted with derision.

'Shouldn't need to replace the regulator. There's no way it should have burnt out like that. I think someone tampered with it.'

'Why would anyone do that?' replied Catz.

'I don't know. Do you have any ideas?' Catz fell

quiet, refusing to answer the Captain's question. The awkward silence that ensued was finally broken by the Doctor.

'Let me take a look,' he offered, 'I might be able to fix it without the need for any trisilicate.' He waved his sonic screwdriver at them. 'I've got my own tools for the job.'

Captain Gomez glanced up at the sky. 'No time,' she announced, grimly, 'we'd never get back to the ship before it gets dark. The days are short on this planet,' she explained.

The Doctor was curious. 'What's the problem with night-time then?' he wondered. Chandra and Gomez exchanged looks, not sure how much to tell the Doctor.

'It's not the night,' began Catz, while the other two crew members hesitated, 'it's what happens...'

'It gets dark, cold and the stars come out?' suggested the Doctor, hopefully.

'Two out of three, Doctor,' Gomez told him, 'now get a move on. We need to find shelter.'

She bustled into the massive white stone memorial and the rest of the party followed her.

'Shelter from what?' demanded the Doctor as he too disappeared inside the memorial.

Catz turned and looked directly at him. 'From the walking dead. It's about to start. When night falls the graves empty and the dead of Mordane walk again!'

Catacombs of Terror

The Doctor could hardly believe his eyes. It was a scene from a hundred horror movies but it was really happening, right in front of him. From the doorway to the memorial the Doctor watched with a mixture of fascination and revulsion as bony hands were thrust out of the ground, followed by whole bodies in various states of decomposition.

For as far as the eye could see the graves of Mordane were giving up their dead and the corpses were on the move. Their clothes hung in rags and the remaining flesh on their bodies hung loose from their frames. Some were little more than animated skeletons, hard bones clattering together as they moved. Others retained some flesh but all seemed unnaturally and unhappily returned to life after a long time dead.

'Impossible,' muttered the Doctor and slipped his glasses on to get a better look. Chandra appeared behind him and grabbed him by the arm.

'We need to move Doctor, before they see us!' Chandra sounded quite frightened and with good reason. Even the Doctor had to admit that it was a horrific sight.

'Might be a bit late for that,' suggested the Doctor, nodding towards the graves. Hundreds of zombies were now moving in just one direction – directly towards the spot where the Doctor and Chandra were standing.

'Quick,' insisted Chandra, 'run!'

Taking his advice, the Doctor ran back inside the monument.

'This way,' called Catz, and disappeared through a dark doorway. The Doctor and Chandra followed and, no sooner had they passed though the doorway than the door slammed shut behind them. For a moment they were in total darkness before a light flared and Catz and the Captain appeared out of the darkness, both holding flaming torches.

'These are the catacombs,' Catz told the Doctor.

The Doctor looked around, a nervous expression on his face.

'Is that really a good place to hide then?' he wondered out aloud. 'Surely catacombs are burial places. If it's corpses we want to avoid, this is probably not the place to be.'

'It's okay – these are empty. Well, mostly empty.' Catz grinned. 'Put it this way – there's a lot more of them out there, than in here!'

The Doctor had read about catacombs on the TARDIS Data Bank during the journey to Mordane.

The small party of humans – and the Doctor – made their way deeper into the dark catacombs. At first the passages, which seemed to have been tunnelled into the bedrock of the hill, were quite wide with periodic cavities on each side in which bodies could be laid to rest.

'Luckily this is one of the earliest sites,' Catz told him in a whisper. 'Most of the poor souls buried here have crumbled to dust. You can't make a zombie out of dust can you?'

The Doctor wasn't so sure about that. He remembered the dust that had threatened him on the Moon – that had been animated by the power of the Eternity Crystal. A weird thought occurred

TARDIS
Data Bank
Places of Burial

A **tomb** is a repository for the remains of the dead. The word usually refers to any enclosed burial chamber of any size. It is a general term that can refer to many different kinds of burial space, including burial vaults, monuments, crypts, mausolea and sarcophagi.

Catacombs are any network of caves, grottos or other subterranean places used for the burial of the dead. The original catacombs were a network of underground burial galleries beneath Rome.

A **grave field** is a phrase used to describe a prehistoric burial ground without any ground level buildings or markers.

A **necropolis** is a large cemetery or burial place. The word comes from the Greek nekropolis which translates as "city of the dead." Although sometimes the word is used to describe modern cemeteries outside large settlements, it is usually used to describe much older burial grounds. Often these are located near the centres of ancient civilizations, in abandoned cities and towns.

A **columbarium** is a building which stores cinerary urns (urns holding cremated remains). These are usually public buildings and places of remembrance.

A **mausoleum** is a building which contains a tomb or other burial chamber. In the past they have often been constructed to contain the remains of a deceased political or religious leader. In more modern terms they have become popular with lesser gentry and nobility. A mausoleum encloses a burial chamber either wholly above ground or within a burial vault below the ground level. This vault would contain the body or bodies, usually sealed inside sarcophagi.

to him – could something similar be happening here? He checked his pocket but the stasis box was still firmly shut. Nothing could get in or out. No power, no influence, no energy, it was completely impossible. And yet the Doctor was sure there was a connection.

Suddenly a bony arm shot out of a wall cavity and skeletal fingers tightened around the Doctor's neck. Gasping for air the Doctor grabbed the forearm bone connected to the hand that was strangling him and wrestled with it. With a horrible crack the arm separated at the elbow from the rest of the attacking skeleton which then collapsed into a pile of disconnected bones. But the skeletal hand gripping his neck held as tight as ever. Catz grabbed a thigh bone from the floor and began hitting the hand, again and again. Finally she managed to dislodge it. The skeletal hand flew through the air, hit the rocky wall and broke into pieces.

The Doctor and Catz could now see that there were a handful of skeletons clambering out of their burial chambers and standing in their path. The Captain and Chandra were further down the tunnel, beyond the skeletons. They were cut off!

'Back the way we came,' ordered the Doctor,

taking charge and grabbing Catz's free hand. He set off so fast she nearly dropped the torch. 'There were some side tunnels back here,' he reminded her, 'maybe we can find another way round to the Captain.'

'It is a bit of a maze down here,' commented the girl, breathless but excited. 'Take the right fork.'

The Doctor led Catz down the tunnel she had indicated and could feel from the downward slope of the rocky floor that they were going deeper into the labyrinth.

Back in the main passageway Captain Gomez and Jitan Chandra were staring in disbelief at the skeletons that had appeared between them and the Doctor and Catz. When the others had retreated back the way they had come, the skeletons had turned on their bony heels and started lumbering towards the Captain. Chandra had tried firing his weapon but the energy bolts seemed to have little effect on the hollow skeletons.

'Why are they so... angry?' wondered Captain Gomez. 'They seem so aggressive, it's as if they hate us.'

'Maybe they do,' replied Jitan, returning his

weapon to his belt. 'Perhaps they resent us because we're properly alive.'

The Captain turned and started to run. 'Whatever else they are, they're not particularly fast. Come on.'

With one last fearful look back at the skeletons Chandra started to follow his Captain, his long legs soon putting some distance between himself and his macabre pursuers. With the Captain holding the torch – the only source of light – it was soon impossible to see any sign of the following skeletons. Only the sound of the brittle click-clacking of bones as the skeletons marched relentlessly though the darkness told Chandra that the dead were still pursuing him.

The Doctor and Catz had been forced to slow down. The tunnel was getting tighter, the roof lower. Catz was okay but the Doctor was now forced to bend almost double to avoid banging his head on the uneven ceiling.

'Are you sure we can get out this way?' he asked, not really expecting a response. To his surprise the young girl not only answered but sounded very confident about her reply.

'It gets really narrow for about ten metres and then opens out,' she told him.

She was about three metres in front of him, crouched down. She had propped the flaming torch up against the passage wall in such a way that it made it impossible for any human to see what she was doing. The Doctor's eyes were not human and he could see that she appeared to be consulting some kind of hand held computer. Why would she have such a device programmed with the details about these catacombs? Who was she? The Doctor was sure the answers would be important but now was not the time to be worrying about it.

Keeping his head down the Doctor shuffled forward to join her but Catz was already moving ahead. Now she was moving on her hands and knees and the Doctor did the same. With Catz holding the torch out in front of her it was now almost impossible for the Doctor to see very much at all. Even Time Lord eyes have their limits. Finally the claustrophobic nightmare was over and the Doctor emerged into a much bigger chamber. In front of him Catz was holding the torch high above her head and looking around her to take in the view.

They were in a massive cave, circular in shape

with a number of passageways of various sizes leading off like spokes from a wheel all around the perimeter. The walls were lined with row after row of burial chambers, and rose twenty metres vertically before they curved in to form the rocky ceiling to the room.

'Where to now?' the Doctor asked Catz, interested to see if she would produce her small laptop. He smiled to himself when she did no such thing. Instead she spun on her heels looking at the various options, as if choosing at random. Finally she pointed at one passageway almost diagonally across the room. 'That one' she said.

'How about this one?' suggested the Doctor pointing to a different exit.

Catz pouted, like a toddler about to have a tantrum. 'No – that one.' Without waiting for any further discussion Catz began crossing the chamber.

The Doctor started to follow her, curious as to what it was that she was looking for. It was becoming clear that this young girl had her own agenda in these catacombs and he was determined to discover her secret.

Suddenly there was a sound of movement from

one of the side passages. The Doctor and Catz froze and exchanged a look. Was it the Captain and Chandra? Or more animated corpses? Something was clanking its way up the passage, something heavy and large.

A moment later a giant figure burst out into the chamber and immediately picked up Catz in one armoured arm.

'No more delay. You must give me the Eternity Crystal now. Or I will kill your companion.'

The Doctor's eyes widened in horror. Somehow the robot Agent had found him.

Standoff

'Wait, wait, wait,' shouted the Doctor, running across to where the Agent was standing. 'Let's not do anything hasty.'

The robot inclined its head to look at the Doctor. 'It has been seven hours and thirty three minutes by the Terran measurements of time since you entered your blue box to fetch me the Crystal,' the Agent announced after a split second's consideration, 'that does not appear to be "hasty" by any definition.'

The Doctor was taken aback. 'Is that some kind of robot joke?'

His appreciation for the design of this creature went up even further. This was a very sophisticated Artificial Intelligence and a very rugged, tough and enduring body. Whoever had constructed it was obviously both a technical genius and a wonderful artist. Who was the creator, he wondered, and why had he made this amazing robot? Perhaps if he could find out something more about the robot it might give him a clue as to what was going on here.

'The Crystal isn't here, it's in the TARDIS,' the Doctor told it, to buy himself – and Catz – some time.

'The blue box?'

'My transport,' nodded the Doctor.

'My scans could not penetrate the interior of your craft,' the robot said, sounding confused. 'There were… conflicting readings and indications of extra-dimensionality.'

'I'm impressed,' confessed the Doctor, 'Not many people see past the outer shell.'

'I am not like any other constructs,' the robot replied, with a hint of pride in its booming metallic voice.

'Let the girl go,' suggested the Doctor, 'and we can talk about this. Perhaps if I knew a little more about you and your quest…'

To the Doctor's relief the robot Agent relaxed its massive arm and Catz hurried to the Doctor's side.

The robot stood in silence, internally considering

the evidence – should it give the Doctor the detailed information he was asking for? Or should he just follow his orders to the letter?

As the robot considered its decision, the Doctor hardly dared breathe.

Elsewhere, deeper in the catacombs, Captain Gomez and first officer Chandra were also holding their breath. They were lying in two of the burial chambers that lined the walls. They had picked two that were opposite each other, so that they could see each other across the narrow passageway. They had a clear view as the animated skeletons that had been pursuing them, clanked and clattered past them. None of these horrors turned their eyeless skulls to either side as they passed, and the two crew members were able to breathe a sigh of relief.

Chandra looked across at his Captain and gestured – should we move? Gomez shook her head and held a single finger up. In his head Chandra counted slowly to sixty; sixty seconds, one minute. The Captain had clearly been counting herself because as he reached sixty he heard movement and saw Gomez swinging her legs out of the alcove in which she had been hiding.

Chandra quickly joined her as she retrieved the flaming torch which she had deposited in a wall sconce. Taking care to move quietly, they began to retrace their steps, putting more and more distance between themselves and the skeletons that had been chasing them.

'We need to find the others,' Gomez whispered. Chandra nodded. 'I think I know where Catz will be heading.'

Gomez turned and raised a quizzical eyebrow.

'Her grandfather is buried here, in these catacombs.'

Gomez snorted angrily. 'I knew it. That child had been manipulating us. How much did she offer you?'

'What are you talking about?' Chandra stuttered, blushing under the stare of burning fury in his Captain's eyes.

'I don't believe in coincidence,' Gomez told him firmly. 'The emergency landing… we could have come down anywhere on the surface of this planet – and yet we managed to land very close to these particular catacombs.'

They moved forward as they talked and were now nearing the entrance to the catacombs.

'Captain, stop, listen!' Chandra pleaded.

Gomez stopped and glared at him. 'Are you going to come clean?' she asked him, pointedly.

Chandra shook his head. 'I though I heard something up ahead. Look!' The man pointed past his Captain's head. Gomez twisted her neck and looked where Chandra was pointing. Something was moving further up the passageway. She raised the torch up higher, to cast its light further. The shuffling figure stumbling towards her was now visible but she wished that it had stayed in the dark. It was another animated corpse but this one was much fresher than the skeletons that had been chasing them before. This was a much more recently deceased man, flesh still clung to the bones and a single dead eyeball hung from one eye socket.

'There are more of them!' screamed Chandra. And now as their eyes adjusted to the darkness beyond the pool of light from their torch they could see that there were more zombie-like creatures behind the front runner. Chandra started to estimate their numbers but soon lost count – there were dozens and more were appearing all the time. They had managed to get inside the catacombs and now they were determined to get to the living. The slow moving but unstoppable creatures were shuffling towards them, arms outstretched.

'Run!' suggested Chandra and turned. Gomez was quickly on his heels as they once again retraced their steps, heading back deeper inside the catacombs. Behind them the zombie-like dead kept coming.

And then Chandra remembered the skeletons that were somewhere ahead of them. They were trapped!

The Doctor and Catz were also trapped; the giant robot Agent stood between them and freedom but, for the moment he had stopped threatening them. To the Doctor's delight he had decided that some information sharing might be a good idea.

'The Eternity Crystal is the centrepiece of a unique piece of advanced technology – a machine for creating life itself,' the robot Agent explained.

'But that's impossible, you can't create life from nothing,' exclaimed the Doctor.

'Nothing is impossible for the Darksmith Collective,' the robot replied.

The Doctor gasped. Catz could see that he was shocked. 'Doctor, what is the Darksmith

Collective?' she asked him.

The Doctor looked at her with serious eyes. 'They're artisans,' he told her, 'they make things. Impossible, wonderful, frightening things from all sorts of mundane and everyday materials.'

Catz shrugged. 'So? Back home we've got whole robot factories that make stuff everyday. Hovercars, Jetpacks, Microwave Cookers, all sorts of things.'

'But not like this. That's manufacturing, what the Darksmiths do is more akin to…' The Doctor hesitated, looking for the right word.

'Art,' suggested the robot Agent.

The Doctor nodded. 'But it's a dark art. It's said that the Darksmiths of Karagula can actually manipulate the physical world itself, taking the raw fabric of reality, breaking it into subatomic particles and then putting them back together in new and original ways. They play with space and matter like a human child playing with wet sand.'

The robot Agent took a step forward, opening its arms wide. 'The Darksmiths created me,' it said proudly.

'And a very beautiful job they did,' the Doctor told the Agent.

'But I was made for a specific mission; to recover

the Eternity Crystal. Brother Varlos took on a job, a commission, to make a device capable of recreating life from dead matter. It was the greatest challenge ever taken by the Darksmith Collective. It took Varlos years but finally he managed to solve the problem. His machine was constructed here, on Mordane.'

The Doctor frowned. There was something that wasn't adding up.

'So Varlos made his machine but then what?'

The robot Agent explained. 'He took the Eternity Crystal, leaving the machine incomplete and uncontrollable. For hundreds of years the Darksmiths have watched and waited for a sign from the Crystal and now, after all that time, it has finally come. We must find the Crystal. We must complete the assignment given to us so long ago.'

Suddenly a piercing scream filled the air.

'Doctor – look!' shouted Catz, her voice trembling with fear. The Doctor looked up and saw the reason for her concern.

They were no longer alone in the chamber. From each doorway dozens of figures were pouring into the room, shuffling and stumbling towards them. The animated dead of the graves of Mordane were coming for them. The Doctor, Catz and the Agent were completely surrounded.

An Empty Grave

n every direction all Catz could see were the horrific reanimated corpses shuffling relentlessly towards them. An eerie low groaning filled the air, a grumbling angry sound that matched the creatures' unstoppable hostility. She moved closer to the Doctor, who put a protective arm around her shoulders.

'Listen to me.' The Doctor was speaking to the robot Agent. 'You've seen my TARDIS – the blue box. There's no way to get inside it, not even the infamous Darksmiths of Karagula can breach the security of the Time Lords of Gallifrey.'

The robot Agent could see where the Doctor's logic was taking him.

'If I want to gain access to your blue box, I need you,' the robot summarised.

'Alive,' added the Doctor, pointedly. The nearest zombies were now just a few metres away, their outstretched hands reaching towards them aggressively.

'Will you help us?' he asked the robot Agent. The metallic creature nodded its head in agreement. The Doctor quickly turned to Catz. 'Right – which exit do we want?'

'Won't any exit do?' she asked.

The Doctor shook his head. 'No more games Catz, I know you've got a map of these catacombs and I know you're looking for something. So choose the best exit and let's get on with it, shall we?'

Realising that the time for secrets might have passed, Catz produced her laptop and quickly consulted the database records of the catacombs. 'We need that exit,' she announced, pointing to a doorway about six metres away. Luckily it was one of the few doorways not filled with zombies but there were about thirty of the shuffling nightmares in their way.

The Doctor looked to the robot. 'I'm assuming you have some kind of weaponry?'

'Of course,' replied the Agent.

'Please, use it with restraint. These creatures are

not hostile themselves. They're victims as much as anything, aren't they?'

The Agent nodded again. 'The Darksmiths tested their device here but it wasn't entirely successful. The device, without the Eternity Crystal is unstable but still functions, repeating the activation signal and bringing the dead back to life.'

'Except they're not alive, are they? There's no cell regeneration, just reanimation of the dead cells of the corpses. That wasn't what Varlos intended was it?'

The robot Agent chose not to answer the question. It turned and raised an arm towards the zombies blocking the Doctor and Catz. Silently a panel opened up along the length of its arm and an energy weapon emerged. The Agent fired his weapon while sweeping his arm in a steady arc. The nearest zombies staggered and fell causing those behind to stumble and fall onto the rocky floor of the cavern. For a moment it was chaos as more zombies moved towards them, as if attracted by the actions of the robot Agent.

'Quick,' called the Doctor and grabbing Catz by the hand he led her round the fallen corpses and out of the chamber into the passageway she had indicated. As they disappeared Catz glanced back and saw that the robot Agent was now almost engulfed in a moving mass of the dead. 'Will it be alright?' she asked the Doctor.

'That thing survived a trip through space hanging on to my TARDIS,' the Doctor told her. 'It's not going to let a few angry animated corpses stop it.'

The passageway was dark and they had managed to leave their flaming torch in the big chamber but the Doctor was able to provide some light, albeit blue-coloured, with his sonic screwdriver. In addition the computer had a backlit screen and between their two pieces of technology they had enough light to navigate by.

'So what are we looking for?' asked the Doctor.

'A grave,' Catz answered.

'Looks like you came to the right place,' commented the Doctor with a smile.

'My grandfather was… buried here,' Catz told him in a strangely quiet voice. 'That's why we came here. I wanted to pay my respects.'

The Doctor said nothing. He knew there was more to this than the girl was telling him but he also knew that she would tell him when she was ready.

'It should be along here,' Catz said.

For the first time the Doctor noticed that each of the burial chambers that lined the passageways of the catacombs was labelled in an alien script – some kind of numbering system. The collection of scratches above each alcove presumably enabled the grieving families to locate their relatives.

'One of these?' asked the Doctor indicating the alcoves.

'No,' Catz replied, 'it's a private chamber. Bigger than these…'

'So all we have to do is translate these symbols,' the Doctor said.

'The only one that's translated on the map, is this one,' Catz said pointing to one of the inscriptions. 'It says "Here Lies Lord Grey Fouston, Rest in Peace".'

'Let's see if we can work out what this one says, then,' the Doctor said.

Activity

Unscramble the codes...

A	B	C	D	E	F	G
○	⊖	⊕	⊙	◐	⊙	)

H	I	J	K	L	M	N
(	∩	⌒	⌣	⌯	△	⌐

O	P	Q	R	S	T	U
∟	Γ	⌐	□	⊟	⊞	↔

V	W	X	Y	Z		
◁	⊔	⊟	⊡	C		

'□□□□ □□□□ □□□□
□□□□ □□□□□□□ □□□□
□□ □□□□□.'

What does this inscription say?
Enter your Answer: _____

_____

'□□□□□□□□ □□□ □□□□□□□□
□□□□ □□□□ □□□□ □□□□□□□
□□ □□□□□□□.'

What does this inscription say?
Enter your Answer: _____

_____

The robot Agent was buried beneath hundreds of the zombie creatures. Dozens of bony hands were scrapping at its metallic skin but the only damage they were doing was to themselves. Nevertheless the increasing weight of the creatures was beginning to worry the Agent. The victims of Varlos' failed test seemed to be angry with anything that had life, even the artificial life of a robot, and to want to snuff any such life out. Even the superior form of the robot could be damaged if the creatures trapped it here.

With a huge effort the robot reared up and swung its limbs to throw the creatures off. Activating its energy weapon it fired in a wide arc, ignoring the Doctor's request, it increased the power. All around the creatures began to disintegrate under the assault from the Agent's advanced weapons. The robot took a step towards the exit that the Doctor and Catz had taken but before it could follow them out more zombies appeared from the other passageways. The robot Agent recharged its weapon systems and prepared to fight once more.

Once the Doctor and Catz had translated the burial chamber, which read 'Sleeping for eternity here lies Lady Rosilie of Peladon', they moved to the next. The chamber that Catz finally led them to was quite different from the previous locations they had seen in the catacombs. It was about ten metres square, with a high ceiling and colourful hangings decorated the walls. In the centre of the room was a large stone sarcophagus and scattered around the room were boxes of jewels and artworks.

'Who was your grandfather?' asked the Doctor amazed.

'King Morrish a'Jethwa,' said Catz simply.

'Of the Folflower Royal Family?'

Catz nodded.

'Which makes you a Princess!' exclaimed the Doctor.

'I wish,' muttered Catz in a far from regal fashion. She was looking for something on the top of the sarcophagus without any success.

'It's not here,' she complained.

'What isn't?' asked the Doctor.

'My inheritance,' replied Catz.

Suddenly Catz was on her feet and heading back towards the passageway.

'Now where?' asked the Doctor.

'Look around Doctor – there's lots of valuable

things here, but they've not been touched. But the torc that I was promised, that's the one thing that's been taken. Why would that be?' Catz answered her own question before the Doctor had a chance to open his mouth. 'I'll tell you. Because someone knew all about it. Someone I trusted. And now they've taken it for themselves, I need to find Jitan Chandra and then I'm going to…' she trailed off.

'What?' asked the Doctor, fearing the worst.

To his surprise the girl just stopped and sat down, tears beginning to fill her eyes. 'I trusted him and now he's betrayed me,' she sobbed, 'and I don't know what to do.'

The torc was golden and seemed to be slightly warm. It glowed with an amazing inner light. 'It's beautiful,' commented Jitan Chandra as the flickering golden glow reflected in his eyes.

'It had better be worth all this trouble,' said Captain Gomez, her face fixed as usual, giving nothing away.

'Only time will tell,' Chandra replied. Gomez was looking at her chronograph. 'Not long until the next dawn,' she told him, 'the dead should be returning to their resting places.'

'Until the next night…' Chandra reminded her.

'By which time we'll be a long way from here. Now let's get moving.'

'What about the others?' Chandra asked, not following his Captain, immediately forcing her to stop and look back at him.

'The girl knows the score. She and that Doctor can find their way back to the ship themselves. Or else they'll join the dead here.'

Catz's Confession

The Doctor sat down next to Catz and put an arm around her shoulders.

'Why don't you start at the beginning,' he suggested, 'and tell me all about it?'

Catz sniffed and wiped at her eyes with the sleeve of her shirt.

'The thing is this is all my fault,' she began, 'the crash landing, everything.'

Slowly, with careful prompting, the Doctor got her to explain her story. Catz was the grand daughter of the late King Morrish a'Jethwa, a monarch who had ruled a collection of five planets in the Folflower system for many years. The King had been a good ruler but there were people who resented the hereditary monarchy and wished for a more democratic leadership. The King, an educated and fair-minded man, had allowed considerable freedom of speech, even allowing his political opponents to meet and plot against him.

On his death his enemies had made their move. Before the late King's son could even think about arranging a coronation, a bloodless coup had taken place and an elected leader took office. The late King's son and his family had been sent into exile.

'So the man who never made it to be King – that was your father?' asked the Doctor when the girl paused in her story. Catz nodded.

'He used to talk to me about the old days all the time,' she continued. 'He really resented being cheated out of his destiny. He was determined that I would do better. He sent me away to the best school in the sector, made sure that I was prepared in every way to be a successful and powerful person. And he always reminded me of my heritage and of my inheritance. He told me about the royal torc that had been handed down by generations in my family.'

The new republican government of the Folflower System had insisted on sending the corpse of the late King to the distant burial world of Mordane, so as not to create a memorial around which forces loyal to the monarchy could gather.'

'Did it work?' asked the Doctor.

'No,' Catz smiled. 'My grandfather and his predecessors were natural leaders, who cared about their worlds and all the people who lived on them. The republicans were more interested in themselves and their own power struggles. Ever since the death of my grandfather things have gone from bad to worse in the Folflower System. People are crying out for the return of the monarchy. My father is too old now, so it's up to me. But I need the torc – it's a symbol of my right to rule.'

'And this piece of jewellery was buried here with your grandfather?' the Doctor asked.

Catz nodded quietly.

'I told Chandra about it. He must have got here first and taken it.'

The Doctor was still confused. 'But why now? Why couldn't your father have come to collect the torc years ago?'

'Because no one knew where Mordane was,' explained Catz, as if it was obvious.

The Doctor was surprised. 'No one knew where it was? How did that happen?' Catz sighed. For someone who seemed to know so much about all sorts of things the Doctor could be really dim sometimes.

'Mordane's been abandoned for decades. It was given a Grade Two Exclusion Order by the Galactic Union,' she told him, patiently, 'no-one comes here anymore, not ever.'

Catz explained that although it had once been the burial planet for a dozen races from more than thirty different worlds, it had been quarantined eighty years ago under mysterious circumstances.

'At the time there was talk of a deadly space plague, a horrible disease that threatened to wipe out billions of lives if it wasn't contained. But no one ever seemed to be very clear about what the disease was, or where it had come from, or even if it could be treated. It was just made clear that no one could ever come here again and, slowly, people forgot about Mordane. All records were erased.'

The Doctor stood up and looked around the tomb at the artefacts that had been buried with the dead king. 'So how did you get to be here?' he wondered.

'My father spent years searching for Mordane, looking for clues, sifting through millions of old commercial space liner flight plans and space navy records from a dozen worlds, trying to identify the missing planet. When I was old enough I continued his work. And I found it! I found a data base which not only told me where the planet was but also gave me a breakdown of the layout of the different areas, right down to maps of individual catacomb systems like this one.'

The Doctor had made his way to the doorway and held a hand to his ear.

'I can hear movement. We need to get out of here.'

Catz got to her feet. 'We just need to keep moving until dawn – for some reason the dead return to their graves when daylight comes.'

'I wonder why that should be?' wondered the Doctor.

'I don't know,' replied Catz, 'does it really matter?'

The Doctor shrugged. 'Who knows?' He started moving off down the passageway taking the route with a slight upward slant. 'We need to get back to the surface and find the others. Don't want them getting back to their ship, making repairs and going off without you, do we?'

Catz grunted. 'Not much chance of that,' she muttered. The Doctor cast her a quick curious glance over his shoulder.

'I sabotaged the ship. Chandra showed me how – I just needed to take out this bit of kit.'

'First officer Chandra told you how to sabotage the ship?' the Doctor was surprised by this new detail.

'He was really nice. At least I thought he was. He talked to me. And he listened too. I told him all about why I really wanted to hire Captain Gomez and her ship. And about the torc.'

'What had you told Gomez?' the Doctor wondered.

'That I was looking for a lost spaceship,' she explained. 'Ouch!' she exclaimed suddenly as she found herself walking directly into the Doctor's back. 'Sorry,' he muttered, realising that he might have stopped a little too quickly, 'but we've got company.'

Looking past the Doctor's arm, Catz could see some animated corpses staggering towards them. Heads at odd angles, arms outstretched, they looked determined to tear Catz and the Doctor into tiny pieces. Quickly Catz turned on her heel and ran. Without looking back she could tell that the Doctor was close behind her.

Even though they were running for their lives

through a dangerous and dark labyrinth over uneven rocky ground the Doctor was still thinking about Catz's story.

'So it was you that sabotaged the spaceship?' he confirmed.

'I hid the trisilicate link on the ship. Chandra was confident that he could make a safe crash landing and he did. He promised me that he'd help me find my inheritance but he's betrayed me.'

'Keep running,' the Doctor reminded her.

Suddenly Catz found herself in another wider chamber, similar to the one in which they had left the robot Agent. She paused and waited for the Doctor who emerged a moment later.

'Use your map,' suggested the Doctor, urgently. 'We need to work out where to go from here.'

Catz pulled the hand held computer from her pocket and flipped it open.

'Oh no,' she cried in dismay.

'What's wrong?' asked the Doctor.

Catz handed the tiny computer to him. 'Look for yourself. Totally security locked.'

'Don't you have a password?' asked the Doctor.

Catz shook her head.

'It has a logic problem you need to crack to gain

access to the main screen,' she explained. 'I don't do logic.'

'Of course you do. Logic's just a way of thinking through a problem in simple stages. One step at a time.'

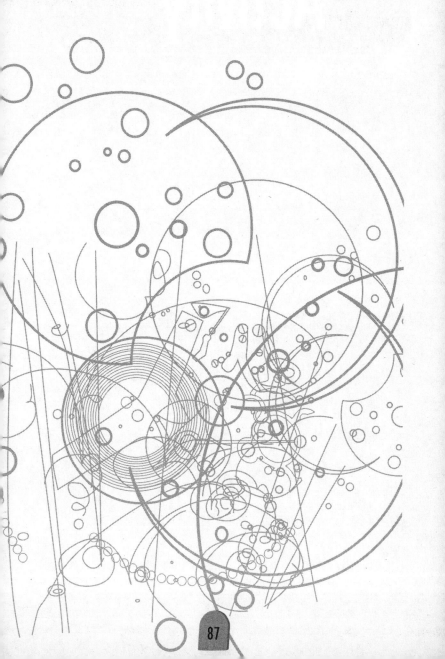

Activity

1. ⋀⋀ 2. ‖‖‖ 3. ☾ 4. ⫽

Which symbol is logically the next in the sequence? Enter your Answer: _____

1. ⊘ 2. ⋀⋀ 3. ‖‖‖ 4. ☾

Which symbol is logically the next in the sequence? Enter your Answer: _____

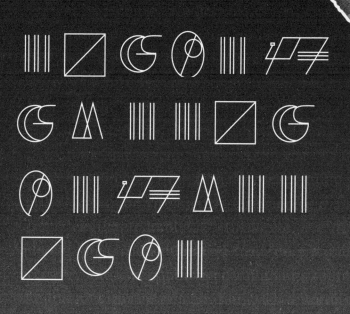

1. ◺ 2. ⦀⦀ 3. ⫽⫽ 4. ◖

Which symbol is logically the next in the sequence? Enter your Answer: _____

Rescue

'That's it!' announced the Doctor, punching in the answer with the tiny keyboard. 'The second one, then the first one and then the third one. Obvious really.'

Instantly the security locks opened and the Doctor was able to access the detailed information about the catacombs. Quickly scanning the data, the Doctor soon found what he was looking for. He began taping what looked like a solid rock wall.

'What are you doing?' asked Catz, sounding confused.

'Looking for something like this,' announced the Doctor as a previously undetectable door of rock suddenly slid open. 'Oh that's beautiful,' he commented, admiring the engineering. 'Look at it,' he continued, 'been here hundreds of years and still in perfect working order. That's amazing.'

Catz was less impressed and more quizzical. 'But what's it for? Why have a hidden door in the catacombs?'

The Doctor was already disappearing into the corridor beyond the door. Catz hurried to keep up with him.

'Remember these catacombs were purpose built, like the temples, and mausolea and memorials and the graveyards. There are buildings on this planet from all sorts of time periods and all sorts of cultures but they are not originals,' the Doctor explained as he moved quickly along the new corridor. Unlike the catacomb passageways this corridor was a smooth-walled, machine-cut tunnel, with recessed ceiling lights at regular intervals.

'In the past there were thousands of funerals here on Mordane every day, and lots of staff needed to run the operation. Like behind the scenes at Disney World, there's a whole lot of stuff here that's completely invisible,' the Doctor continued.

'What's Disney World?' demanded Catz.

The Doctor was spared a long explanation as they reached what appeared to be a dead end. Catz sighed but the Doctor just grinned. 'Give me a chance,' he said and pulled out his sonic screwdriver. After a quick adjustment he activated the device and the wall in front of them slid open and they were able to walk into the outside air.

Catz took a deep breath and spread her arms wide. 'At last,' she smiled, 'I was beginning to think I'd never see the outside world again.'

The Doctor grabbed her hand. 'Unfortunately there are some things out here I wasn't in a hurry to see again!'

Catz looked around and could see what the Doctor meant. They had lost track of time in the catacombs and it was still night and, as she looked around in every direction, she could see shapes moving in the darkness. Shapes of corpses. The dead of Mordane were still walking.

'Incredible,' muttered the Doctor. 'Somehow it's as if they can sense us. As if they know we're really alive and all they have is a mockery of life.'

Catz couldn't believe the Doctor was just standing there doing nothing. 'Doctor – I don't care about the whys. I just don't want them to get hold of us.'

The stumbling, shuffling creatures were now getting quite close. It was a horrific sight – the dead creatures, limbs bent and awkward, moving slowly but determinedly towards them in near silence. The Doctor and Catz were now back to back, circling slowly. In every direction they could see only more and more zombies. Suddenly there was a new sound, a high-pitched buzzing, that seemed to be coming from a long way off.

The Doctor inclined his head and listened. The sound was getting louder. Suddenly there was a light in the sky above them. Catz looked up and shouted in delight. 'It's a rescue party!'

A powerful spotlight from above caught them in a circle of intense light and a rope ladder dropped down towards them. Catz quickly scrambled onto the ladder and the Doctor followed her. The rescue had come in the nick of time. Even as the helicopter began to rise the nearest of the zombies was reaching for the bottom of the rope ladder. Its bony fingers tried to grab hold of the final rung but it couldn't get a firm grip and the Doctor and Catz were carried clear of the throng of angry corpses.

The Doctor hurried up the ladder and climbed inside the helicopter where Catz was waiting for him with Captain Gomez.

'Thought you could use a lift,' smiled the Captain.

The Doctor looked around at the helicopter.

'You went back to your ship?'

'What about the dead? Didn't they try and stop you?' asked Catz.

'They couldn't touch us,' said Gomez smiling broadly. She held up a shimmering yellow glowing torc. 'This protected us.'

Halfway across the galaxy, on the remote planet Karagula, High Minister Drakon, the leader of the Darksmith Collective, was impatiently awaiting an answer from Sister Maggen. He repeated the question, his husky rasping voice echoing around the rocky chamber where the high council held their meetings.

'Has the signal from the Crystal been located again?'

Sister Maggen shook her head. 'No. There's been nothing since it first disappeared.'

'Varlos!' hissed Drakon. When the emissions from the Crystal had disappeared so completely the Darksmiths had assumed that it must have been the work of the traitor Varlos - the Darksmith genius who had first made the Crystal. The Darksmiths had no idea that the Doctor had placed the Crystal in a stasis box, cutting it off completely from the rest of the Universe.

'And no word from our Agent either?'

Brother Ardos stepped forward. 'The shuttle pod has returned on automatic recall. The Agent was not on board.'

Drakon was not pleased by the news. This had been their first chance in centuries to retrieve the lost Crystal and fulfil their long delayed contract but now it seemed to be slipping through their fingers.

'Where is the Agent now?'

Ardos hesitated, knowing that the news would not be received well. 'According to the automatic signal transmissions, he has travelled by some means unknown to the planet Mordane.'

High Minister Drakon took a sharp intake of breath. 'Mordane! That cannot be a coincidence!'

'Perhaps Varlos has taken the Crystal back to the place it was first tested?' speculated Sister Maggen.

Drakon's face was grave. 'That test was a disaster. The planet has been quarantined ever since. We should have destroyed Varlos' device. If the Crystal is reunited with...' He trailed off, unable to complete the sentence. They all knew the consequences if the prototype machine Varlos had created on Mordane was fully activated again. It would be a disaster on an unimaginable scale – the reanimated dead would walk on a million worlds.

'The Agent must succeed in his mission,' insisted Drakon sombrely, 'for the sake of the entire Universe!'

The Doctor had quickly helped Captain Gomez and first officer Chandra re-install the trisilicate link that Catz had hidden and reactivated the engine thrust regulator. Having made that repair they then quickly checked the rest of the spacecraft's systems and soon declared the ship fit for use again.

The Doctor found Catz sitting on a spare seat on the Bridge, looking at the torc. 'Beautiful, isn't it,' she murmured, aware of the Doctor joining her.

'And so useful too,' agreed the Doctor. 'Who would have guessed that something so small could generate such a powerful personal protection shield?'

'Good job it did, or the Captain and Chandra would never have made it back through the graveyards to the ship to get the helicopter out. Thanks for getting it for me.'

Chandra, who had been programming the launch

sequence turned and gave her a smile. 'My pleasure,' he told her, 'when the Captain and I stumbled into the tomb you told me about I thought I should take it while I could.'

'But not for yourself, for me,' Catz returned the smile. 'I'm sorry I ever doubted you.'

'No harm done,' replied Chandra. 'Just remember me when you get the rest of your inheritance.'

The Doctor looked at Catz with serious eyes. 'Are you sure you want to be a ruler? It's not an easy job, you know.'

'I have a duty,' Catz told him.

The Doctor nodded. 'As do I,' he announced. 'I need to do something about these zombies. And I need your help.'

'Haven't we done enough?' It was Captain Gomez, standing in the doorway to the Bridge and looking grim. 'The days are short here Doctor and in a couple of hours the dead will walk again. That pretty necklace might protect one or two of us, but the rest of us won't be so lucky.'

The Doctor turned to her. 'Please, it won't take very long, but I cannot do it alone.'

Catz stood up next to the Doctor. 'I'm still paying for this trip, aren't I?' Gomez nodded. 'In that case I want to help the Doctor. So, what do we need to do?'

All eyes turned to the Doctor.

'These aren't zombies,' he explained, 'they're not the dead coming to life; they're just dead matter being animated by something else. I saw something similar on the Moon – dust made into a semblance of life.'

'What is the force that's animating them, then?' asked Gomez.

The Doctor pulled out a small box from his pocket. 'Inside here is a powerful Crystal,' he said, 'a Crystal that was made by the Darksmiths of Karagula. There's a machine here, a device that was powered by this Crystal. It went wrong and has been malfunctioning ever since but I think if I reconnect the Crystal and reprogram the device I can turn off the signal.'

The Doctor looked around at the faces of the three humans. 'I just need your help to find the machine.'

Reverse the Polarity

I t was the database on Catz's little handheld
computer that eventually gave the vital clue. Scans
using the spaceship's sensors failed to locate the
device Varlos had made but a careful examination
of the information held on Catz's machine revealed
a series of a dozen administrative towers placed at
various locations around the small planet. After
that it was a process of elimination to find the right
one. The process took almost all day.

Jitan Chandra piloted the helicopter to take the
Doctor and Catz back across the graveyards to the
tower that they had identified. As the helicopter
gently touched down on the ground, the Doctor
could see that the shadows were getting rather long
again. Daylight was slipping away.

'You've got about thirty minutes,' Chandra

told his passengers. 'Once it's dark the dead will walk again.'

'Not if we're successful,' the Doctor reminded him, cheerfully.

Chandra looked around nervously. 'Nevertheless if it gets dark I'll have to leave you and get back to the ship.'

Catz bit her lip and looked a bit nervous. Chandra saw her expression and gave her a reassuring smile. 'You've got your torc, haven't you? But it can't protect me and the copter. If you need more time I'll go back to the ship and come back for you at dawn. Don't worry.'

'It won't come to that,' the Doctor assured him. 'Once I get this hooked up it won't take a jiffy to reverse the signal.' The Doctor sounded confident but then ruined it. 'Well, maybe a couple of jiffys,' he added, 'three jiffys at the most. Whatever that is. Actually I'm not really sure what a jiffy is.'

Catz sighed. 'Whatever it is, it's going to take a lot of them if we don't get a move on. Come on.'

The Doctor and Catz jumped out of the helicopter and, keeping their heads down, ran across to the entrance to the tower. It was an impressive building – tall and elegant, slightly organic in style. The

Doctor's sonic screwdriver made short work of the locked door and they were soon able to get make their way inside.

It wasn't difficult to find the device that the Darksmith Varlos had constructed. It almost filled a large chamber in the middle of the hollow interior of the building. Above the mysterious machine cables rose high into the air, attached to various galleries that spiralled up the inside of the circular tower. In the middle of the alien device was a circular chamber centred on a dais with five similarly shaped receptacles.

The Doctor took the stasis box out of his pocket and activated the hidden controls that would open it. The lid slowly opened and the Eternity Crystal was revealed, sparkling in the light. Carefully the Doctor picked the Crystal up and looked at the five crystal-shaped receptacles.

'Which one?' wondered Catz.

Activity

Where should the Crystal go?

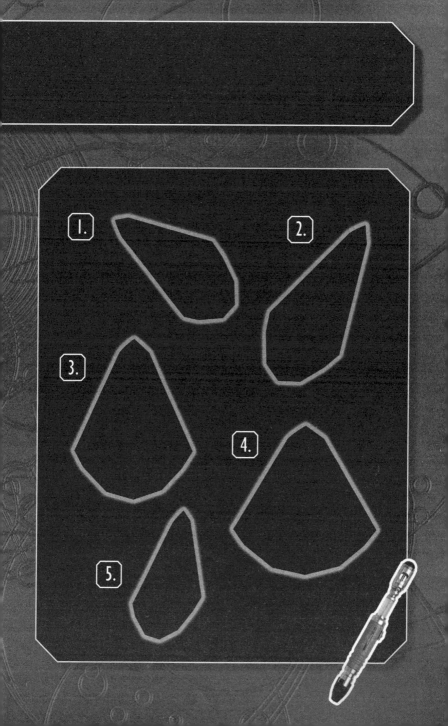

The Doctor considered for a moment and then placed the Crystal into the third possible resting place. Immediately, clamping arms emerged from the surface of the dais to grip the Crystal firmly. Lights and dials on the surrounding equipment flashed in response to the return of the Eternity Crystal. The Crystal itself began to pulse with a deep blue light.

On distant Karagula, Brother Ardos of the Darksmith Collective found his sensitive instruments also reacting. Immediately he ran to find High Minister Drakon.

'The Eternity Crystal has appeared again,' he announced, breathlessly when he managed to track down Drakon.

'Where?' asked Drakon simply.

'Mordane,' Ardos told him.

'Is our Agent still on Mordane?'

Ardos nodded. High Minister Drakon smiled coldly. 'Then it is just a matter of time. Our Agent is unstoppable. It will detect the Crystal's emissions. There is no force in the Universe that can stop it completing the mission. The Eternity Crystal will soon be ours again.'

On the surface of Mordane in Sector Alpha night fell. Immediately the dead world began to come to life, as it had done every night for centuries. Hands burst through the ground and corpses pulled themselves from their resting places. Tombs creaked open and partly decayed bodies emerged. Catacombs and mausolea disgorged stumbling, staggering figures as the dead of Mordane reclaimed their world once again. As if sensing the life in the tower and the threat they represented, the massed army of the dead converged on that location.

Chandra, sitting in the pilot's seat of the helicopter, took one look at the hordes of animated corpses emerging from every direction and fired up the engines. Although the zombies were slow moving their sheer numbers made a rapid exit necessary and Chandra lost no time in getting the chopper into the air and heading back towards the relative safety of the spaceship. As he flew away from the Doctor and Catz, he prayed that they would complete their mission quickly. Surely the Doctor had said it wouldn't take much time at all. What had gone wrong?

Catz watched as the Doctor scurried around the

alien machine, adjusting controls, flicking switches, checking readouts. 'How much longer?' she asked in a worried tone. She glanced at her watch and noted, with a slight panic, that the thirty minutes Chandra had given them were all but gone.

'This machine is incredible,' the Doctor told her, 'a work of real genius. I just need to realign the input/output system and then,' he paused and grinned, 'I just have to reverse the polarity of the neutron flow.'

The Doctor made another adjustment with his sonic screwdriver. 'Well, I say the neutron flow, but it's not really a neutron flow, it's more a hyper-sonic animating pulsar, but you know what I mean.'

'Not really,' confessed Catz.

'Basically I do this,' the Doctor announced, pulling down a large lever, 'and everything gets reversed.'

Above the sound of the machine, Catz thought she heard something else, a sound of movement. Was it Chandra looking for them? 'Doctor?' she began and then stopped as she realized the terrible truth. The sound she could hear was the sound of shuffling reanimated corpses. It was still happening. The dead were still walking and they were coming for her.

The Doctor had heard it too. 'Why isn't it

working?' Catz demanded. The Doctor didn't answer immediately. He was too busy going over all the dials and readouts.

'Something's wrong,' he muttered, 'there's something we haven't thought about.' The Doctor threw back his head and looked up, carefully following the trail of cables as they stretched up towards the distant roof. 'There!' he exclaimed. 'These cables... they're taking the signal to some kind of satellite dish but for some reason it isn't getting through.'

The Doctor looked back at the control panels. 'Got it!' he exclaimed suddenly. Catz hurried across to him and looked at the screen where he was pointing. 'There's a distributor box overloading,' the Doctor explained, calling up a graphic showing the layout of the device. 'With a bit of luck I can fix that with the sonic,' he told her, starting to move away from the controls.

Catz followed him towards the entrance, casting a last look back at the Eternity Crystal rhythmically flashing blue in its position at the heart of the machine. The Doctor seemed to have memorised the map as he was able to take a series of left and right turns down various corridors to reach his goal. Suddenly he stopped dead. Catz looked past him and saw the reason. Ahead of them a dozen or more zombies filled the corridor, stumbling towards them with deadly intent.

'The distributor box is at the end of the corridor,' the Doctor told her urgently.

'Give me the sonic' Catz insisted. 'I can use my torc and walk straight through them.'

The Doctor shook his head. 'Give me the shield. I'll do it.'

Catz was determined to do it though. 'It's my fault we're here. I need to make things right. Let me do this.'

The Doctor could see that she was not going to give up. Quickly he demonstrated the controls of the sonic screwdriver and handed it over to the brave young girl.

Catz took the sonic device and activated the force field generator hidden inside the torc she had inherited from her grandfather. Inside the force field there was a tiny hum that told her that it was active. Nothing could touch her inside the force field. Quickly she ran towards the approaching zombies.

She had never been quite so close to them before. Up close they were even more disgusting.

At this distance she could see the details of their decaying flesh, see the bones of the skeletons where decomposition was at a greater stage. As she got even closer the zombies herded towards her, arms reaching out for her with bony fingers extended.

The force field held, repelling the attacking corpses, who bounced off the invisible protective bubble like balls bouncing off a wall. Now she was in the midst of them, surrounded on all sides by the terrifying creatures. Determinedly she kept walking, taking small steps but kept moving.

The zombies tried but could not find a way to grip the force field. Catz closed her eyes and pushed on. When she opened her eyes again a moment later she was through. Now the corpses were between her and the Doctor. The zombies gave up on Catz and turned, stumbling towards the Doctor. Catz glanced back and was shocked to see the Doctor standing his ground.

'Go on!' he urged her.

Catz didn't need to be told twice. She reached the distribution box and deactivated the force field. Then she pointed the sonic screwdriver at the box, as the Doctor had instructed her, and pressed the button.

Win, Lose

There was a long pause. Nothing seemed to happen. Catz turned back and looked towards the Doctor. It was almost impossible to see him now. The animated corpses were nearly upon him. Another moment and they would reach him and tear him apart. Catz looked back at the distribution box. Had it worked? Was the signal getting through?

'Come on!' she whispered and then a familiar blue glow seemed to pass through the distribution box. The cable coming out of the box also glowed blue. Was this the Eternity Crystal's energy taking the reversed signal to the broadcast aerials high on the tower?

'Oh yes!' cried a familiar voice behind her. Catz turned and saw an incredible sight. The zombies were collapsing and decaying and, beyond them, the Doctor was jumping up and down in delight.

'It's working!' he beamed at her, as the corpses that a moment ago had been threatening his life crumbled into dust.

'But why are they turning to dust?' asked Catz.

The Doctor told her that the corpses had been maintained in a partial stasis by the original experiment by Varlos. 'The test of the machine didn't entirely work,' he explained. 'It was meant to create life, but all it did was to delay total death. That's why they only became animated at night. They've been reacting to a reflection of the original signal, bouncing off a Darksmiths' satellite in orbit.'

'But it's over now. No more walking dead?' Catz asked nervously.

The Doctor smiled. 'All safe now. Mordane can go back to being a peaceful memorial planet, a worthy place for people to bury their dead.'

'So we won,' Catz checked.

'Looks like it,' he confirmed.

The Doctor and Catz made their way outside. It was dark but for once the planet surface was peaceful and quiet. The only sound was the gentle throb of the helicopter engines as Chandra came to pick them up.

The Doctor declined the offer of a lift. 'I'll make my own way back to the TARDIS,' he told them. 'But first I need to deal with that Crystal.'

'What are you going to do?' asked Chandra.

The Doctor shrugged, a grim expression on his face. 'I don't know but it's too powerful to ignore. I'll just have to try and find a way to destroy it. Power like that is too dangerous. It animated dust on the Moon, it made the dead walk here on Mordane... that's a power that could be terrible in the wrong hands.'

Chandra shook the Doctor's hand and wished him luck. Catz gave him a quick hug, and then turned red with embarrassment. Moments later the Doctor watched as the helicopter took off into the night sky and disappeared into the darkness.

The Doctor turned on his heel and headed back inside the tower. The sooner that Crystal was back in the stasis box the better. He hurried through the lower floor of the tower at a run, heading for the control centre where he had left the Eternity Crystal at the heart of Varlos' terrible machine.

As soon as he came through the doorway to

the inner area he realized something was wrong. The light levels had fallen and the blue glow from the Crystal itself was entirely absent. The Doctor stopped in his tracks and looked in horror at the dais. The Crystal was gone.

On Karagula, High Minister Drakon awaited confirmation from Brother Ardos. The supra-lightspeed shuttle pod had been dispatched under automatic guidance to meet the Agent on Mordane. At any moment confirmation that the mission had been a success should come through.

Ardos crouched over a display unit located inside an outcrop of rock. He turned to Drakon with a cry of delight. 'The shuttle pod is returning,' he announced.

Drakon needed more. 'But is it empty or is the Agent on board?' he demanded.

'The Agent is in the craft,' confirmed Ardos, 'and he has the Eternal Crystal with him. We are detecting its emissions.'

Drakon smiled. 'At last!' he whispered. 'At last we can complete our greatest work.'

The Doctor was used to running. Usually he was

running *from* things, often angry, deadly things but right now he was running *to* something – the TARDIS. The disappearance of the Crystal had shocked him but there was only one possible explanation. The robot Agent had escaped from the catacombs and taken the Crystal.

The Doctor forced himself to keep running at top speed. Finally with his lungs bursting and both hearts pumping like crazy he reached the TARDIS. Quickly he unlocked the door and stumbled in on his aching legs. He hurried to the console and activated the scanners.

'Come on, come on,' he muttered trying to encourage the TARDIS' systems to do the impossible but it was no good. There was no trace of the robot Agent or the Crystal's strange emissions on Mordane. The Agent and the Crystal had vanished completely.

The Doctor knew that the Crystal was dangerous. Too dangerous to be left with the Darksmiths. There was only one thing he could do.

The Doctor swallowed. There weren't many places in the Universe that frightened him but Karagula, home of the Darksmith Collective was one of them. Even when the Time Lords had been able to go to places in force they had never approached Karagula. Now he was the last of the Time Lords and he would have to face the Darksmiths alone.

His face dark with shadows, the Doctor entered the co-ordinates into the TARDIS guidance systems. With a quick pump of the bicycle pump, a final adjustment to the temporal buffers and a thump on the spatial drift circuits with his rubber tipped mallet the Doctor pulled the dematerialisation lever and set his space and time craft in motion.

'Next stop Karagula,' he announced to no-one in particular. 'I just hope this will be a return trip...'

To Be Continued...

To find out what events lie in store
for the Doctor and the mystery of the
Darksmith Legacy, look out for
The Colour of Darkness.
But for now, here is a taste of
things to come...

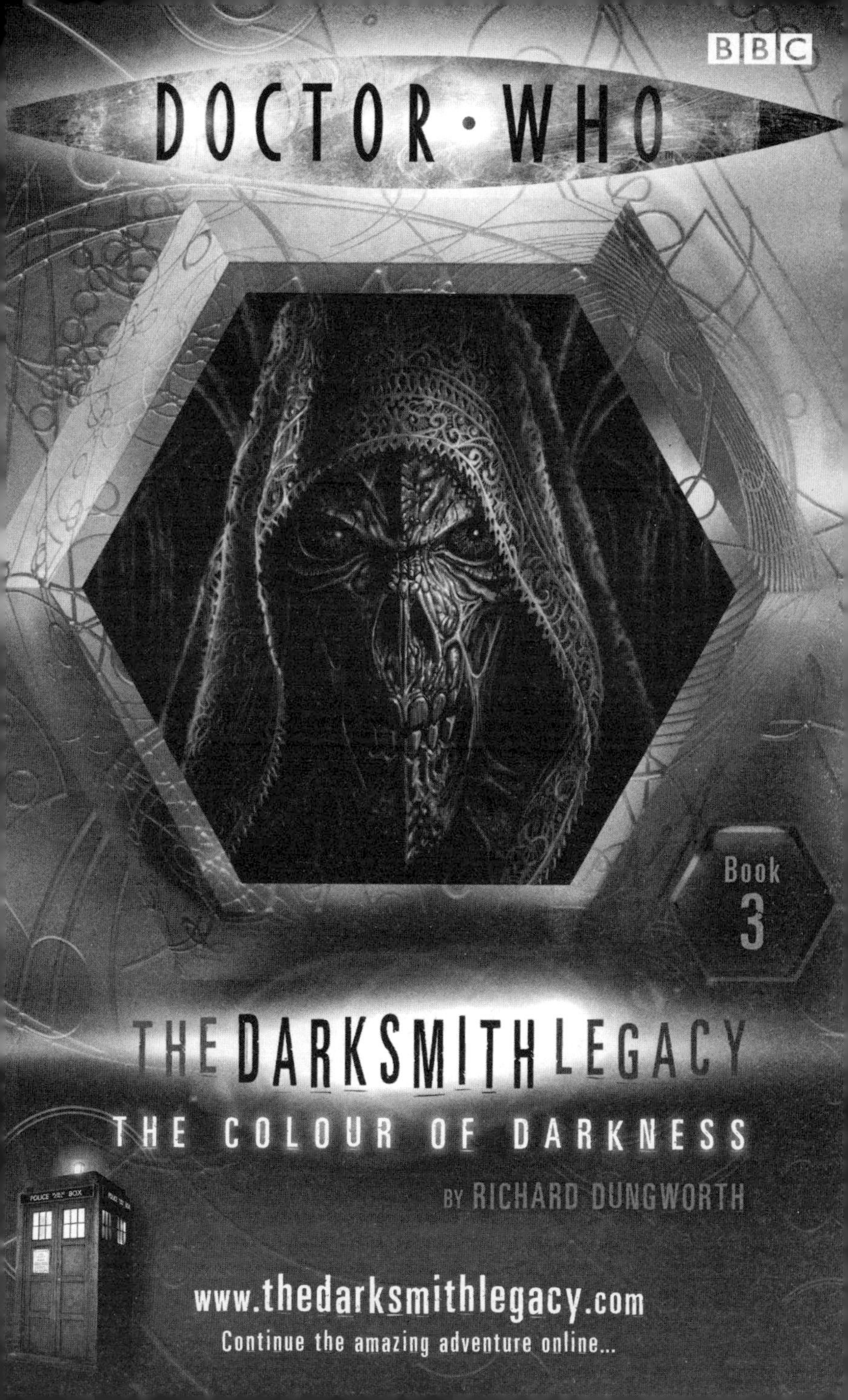
BBC
DOCTOR WHO
Book 3
THE DARKSMITH LEGACY
THE COLOUR OF DARKNESS
BY RICHARD DUNGWORTH
www.thedarksmithlegacy.com
Continue the amazing adventure online...

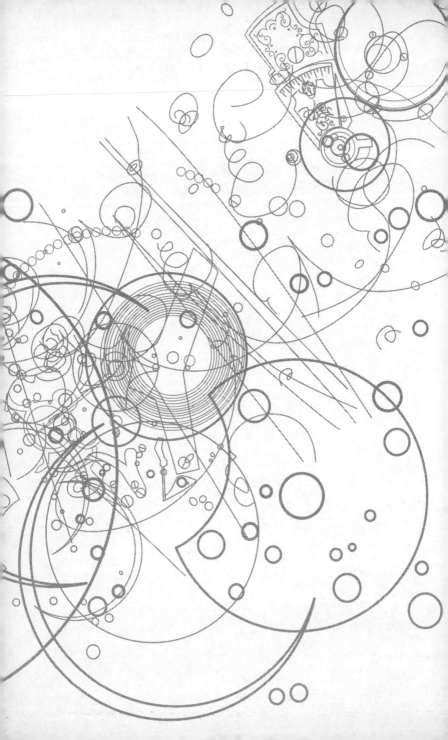

A Price to Pay

Fra' Vallir strode gratefully into the shade of the council hall's arching canopy. At this time of day, the glare of Karagula's twin suns was too intense to bear for more than a few minutes at a time. Even the short walk from his own canopied quarters had left the back of Vallir's neck prickling and his brain half-baked. Normally the entire village would rest through the midday burn. But today Vallir and the other councillors had business to conclude.

He stepped lightly onto the council hall's floating platform, and headed for the pair of beaten-out alloy panels that formed the double-doors of the assembly chamber. He paused for a moment in front of them, feeling anxiety swell in his stomach.

What outcome would this meeting with the

witch-woman have? What would her price be? It had been foolish of the council not to have agreed on a fee *before* accepting her bizarre offer.

But then, thought Vallir, not one of us believed for a moment that she could actually…

Pushing the doors aside, he entered the assembly chamber. The other eleven councillors were already present, seated around the chamber's horseshoe-shaped table. Vallir made his way to his own chair, between those of the council secretary, Fra' Sagral, and the treasurer, Fra' Tramlor.

Sagral, whose dead wife has returned to him. And Tamlor, whose daughter's sightless eyes now see. How can such things come to pass?

He sat, and gave a nod to an attendant standing at the chamber's side entrance. The clerk drew aside its scrap-mesh curtain and ushered in a young, dark-haired woman. She crossed to sit on the bench encircled by the council table.

During her previous visit to the council hall a few days ago, Vallir had been struck by the woman's unusual beauty. There was a rich, misty softness about her, almost as though one's eyes could not quite bring her into focus. She wore the same simple, pale blue robe and meek expression now as she had that day.

But Vallir's opinion of her was utterly changed. This woman had powers he could not comprehend. She was as dangerous as she was beautiful, he was sure. And the council was in her debt.

He cleared his throat.

'You seek an audience with us, madam?'

'Yes, Chief Councillor.' The woman's voice had a hypnotic lilt. 'I trust you are satisfied that I have fulfilled my part of our contract?'

Vallir shuffled awkwardly.

'You have done as you said you would.'

'Then the time has come, I believe, for me to name a price for my services.' She absently fingered a small stone pendant that hung at her neck. 'I have friends who would be unhappy to see me swindled.'

'The integrity of this council is not in question. We made an agreement under Lithic Oath, and it will be honoured.'

'Very well. Then I shall name my price.'

The woman paused, then continued matter-of-factly.

'Your children. My price is your children.'

DOCTOR · WHO

THE DARKSMITH LEGACY

'Collected' Party

Celebrate the epic Darksmith Legacy experience with an out-of-this-world party to be held in a secret London location during the October half-term 2009, after the final exciting instalment has been published.

For your chance to win an exclusive ticket to this Doctor Who Extravaganza you must sign up at www.thedarksmithlegacy.com, complete the quest online and submit your details. We will let you know if you have been successful via email.

This will be a once in a lifetime opportunity to win lots of Doctor Who prizes and see scary monsters up-close...

...Don't miss out!

More party details will be revealed in another dimension on the Darksmith website so keep checking back for further updates. Full Terms and Conditions can also be found at www.thedarksmithlegacy.com.

DOCTOR · WHO

Fantastic free Doctor Who slipcase offer when you buy two Darksmith Legacy books!

Limited to the first 500 respondents!

To be eligible to receive your free slipcase, fill in your details on the form below and send along with original receipt(s) showing the purchase of two Darksmith Legacy books. The first 500 correctly completed forms will receive a slipcase.

Offer subject to availability. Terms and conditions apply. See overleaf for details.

DOCTOR · WHO

THE DARKSMITH LEGACY

www.thedarksmithlegacy.com
Continue the exciting adventure online™

Here
- -

Entry Form

Name: ....

Address: ....

Email: ....

Have you remembered to include your two original sales receipts? ⬡

I have read and agree to the terms and conditions overleaf. ⬡

Tick here if you don't want to receive marketing communications from Penguin Brands and Licensing. ⬡

Important – Are you over 13 years old?

If you are 13 or over just tick this box, you don't need to do anything else. ⬡

If you are under 13, you must get your parent or guardian to enter the promotion on your behalf. If they agree, please show them the notice below.

Notice to parent/guardian of entrants under 13 years old

If you are a parent/guardian of the entrant and you consent to the retention and use of the entrant's personal details by Penguin Brands and Licensing for the purposes of this promotion, please tick this box. ⬡

Name of parent/guardian: ....

Terms and Conditions

1. This promotion is subject to availability and is limited to the first 500 correctly completed respondents received.
2. This promotion is open to all residents aged 7 years or over in the UK, with the exception of employees of the Promoter, their immediate families and anyone else connected with this promotion. Entries from entrants under the age of 13 years must be made by a parent/guardian on their behalf.
3. The Promoter accepts no responsibility for any entries that are incomplete, illegal or fail to reach the promoter for any reason. Proof of sending is not proof of receipt. Entries via agents or third parties are invalid.
4. Only one entry per person. No entrant may receive more than one slipcase.
5. To enter, fill in your details on the entry form and send along with original sales receipt(s) showing purchase of two Doctor Who: The Darksmith Legacy books to: Doctor Who Slipcase Offer, Brands and Licensing, 80 Strand, London, WC2R 0RL.
6. The first 500 correctly completed entries will receive a slipcase.
7. Offer only available on purchases of Doctor Who: The Darksmith Legacy books.
8. Please allow 31days for receipt of your slip case.
9. Slip cases are subject to availability. In the event of exceptional circumstances, the Promoter reserves the right to amend or foreclose the promotion without notice. No correspondence will be entered into.
10. All instructions given on the entry form, form part of the terms and conditions.
11. The Promoter will use any data submitted by entrants for only the purposes of running the promotion, unless otherwise stated in the entry details. By entering this promotion, all entrants consent to the use of their personal data by the Promoter for the purposes of the administration of this promotion and any other purposes to which the entrant has consented.
12. By entering this promotion, each entrant agrees to be bound by these terms and conditions.
13. The Promoter is Penguin Books Limited, 80 Strand, London WC2R 0RL.

Cut Here

Doctor Who Slipcase Offer
Brands and Licensing
80 Strand
London
WC2R 0RL